THE CRICKET WARRIOR
A Chinese Tale

Retold by **Margaret and Raymond Chang**
Illustrated by **Warwick Hutton**

Margaret K. McElderry Books
New York
Maxwell Macmillan Canada
Toronto
Maxwell Macmillan International
New York Oxford Singapore Sydney

TO DEBORAH, MARILYN, JANE, ROBIN, AND CINDY

For JESSICA AND LUCIA
—W.H.

Text copyright © 1994 by Margaret and Raymond Chang
Illustrations copyright ©1994 by Warwick Hutton

Margaret K. McElderry Books
Macmillan Publishing Company
866 Third Avenue, New York, NY 10022

Maxwell Macmillan Canada, Inc.
1200 Eglinton Avenue East, Suite 200
Don Mills, Ontario M3C 3N1

Macmillan Publishing Company is part of the Maxwell Communication Group of Companies.
First edition
Printed in Singapore on recycled paper.
10 9 8 7 6 5 4 3 2 1
The text of this book is set in Zaph Calligraphic.
Library of Congress Cataloging-in-Publication Data
Chang, Margaret Scrogin.
The cricket warrior : a Chinese tale / by Margaret and Raymond Chang ; illustrated by Warwick Hutton.
— 1st ed.   p.   cm.
Summary: In order to save his family, a Chinese boy turns into a fighting cricket and becomes the emperor's champion.
ISBN 0-689-50605-8
[1. Folklore—China.]   I. Chang, Raymond.   II. Hutton, Warwick, ill.
PZ8.1.C3584Cr 1994
398.21—dc20
[E]
93-35395

A long time ago, in China, the emperor loved to watch cricket fights. He ordered a new tax to be paid by everyone—paid with crickets. From north to south, fathers stayed up all night hunting crickets, and children pretended to be great cricket warriors. People who couldn't catch crickets had to buy them, so crickets became very valuable.

Far from the imperial palace lived Cheng Ming, a farmer whose crops had failed for three years in a row because there was so little rain. He had no money left to pay his taxes. On the first day of autumn, the magistrate was going to put him in jail and take away the farm his family had owned for generations. His wife, Li hua, and son, Wei nian, would be turned out on the street to beg.

Their only hope was to capture a fighting cricket. Every day, as he watered spindly wheat sprouts, Cheng Ming searched the furrows and listened for a cricket song.

One evening, while Cheng Ming and Wei nian weeded their small garden, a cricket song throbbed in the still, warm twilight.

"Quick, Wei nian," Cheng Ming whispered. "Fetch a cup of water and a bamboo tube."

Wei nian returned to find his father kneeling beside a mound of dirt, listening hard. Cheng Ming seized the cup and poured water into the soft earth. At once a huge cricket leaped high. Cheng Ming caught it between his hands and forced it into the bamboo tube.

Overjoyed, Wei nian's father said, "Its chest is huge, and its tail is very long, so it must be a good fighter."

Wei nian wished he'd gotten a good look at the cricket.

"You must tell the magistrate immediately," Wei nian's mother said. "Perhaps he'll want to see the cricket this very night."

While Cheng Ming set off for the magistrate's house, Li hua hurried to sweep the courtyard, leaving Wei nian alone with the cricket.

Just one peek, he thought—and he unplugged the bamboo tube. Before he could stop it, the cricket had jumped free and flown out the window.

Wei nian ran crying to his mother.

"You foolish boy," she wailed. "You've lost our only hope."

Sobbing, Wei nian stumbled into the garden, following the cricket.

The cricket's song echoed from the pomegranate grove across the canal. Wei nian ran over the bridge, through the grove, and into the fields beyond, following its call. Tears blurred his eyes. He crawled over strange fields, digging into dry earth, hoping to find the cricket.

Late at night, he collapsed on the ground.

"What is the trouble, my son?"

Wei nian lifted his head to see an old man standing close by. His gown shimmered in the moonlight.

The man's face was kind, so Wei nian told his story. "I have betrayed my family," he said, weeping. "I would do anything to get the cricket back!"

"Would you take its place?" the old man asked.

"If only I could."

Cheng Ming returned home with good news. "The magistrate will come tomorrow morning to test our cricket warrior. If it proves worthy, he will send it to the emperor."

When Li hua told him what Wei nian had done, his joy turned to anger and fear. He called for his son. There was no answer. Cheng Ming and Li hua searched up and down the canal. They crossed the bridge, chased shadows in the pomegranate grove, calling Wei nian's name until their voices were hoarse.

Finally they came home again, hoping to find Wei nian there. But his bed was empty.

At dawn a joyous "Chir-rup! Chir-rup! Chir-rup!" came from the garden, and a small cricket hopped over the threshold. When Cheng Ming reached down to catch it, it jumped into his palm. Exhausted and numb with grief he stared at its burnished red shell, its long neck and strong wings.

At that moment the magistrate arrived. A servant carried his prize cricket, Crabshell Blue, in an ivory cage. Another servant held a fighting bowl.

"Show me your great cricket warrior," the magistrate demanded.

Cheng Ming dropped the little cricket into the fighting bowl. He could not think what else to do. The cricket waved its antennae, trying to look fierce.

"How dare you waste my time with such a puny cricket!" the magistrate shouted. "Take this man to jail *now*!" he ordered his guards.

"Your Honor, please give it a chance." Because he was terrified, Cheng Ming made an empty boast. "It is small, but very fierce."

"Fierce, is it? We'll see about that." The magistrate lowered Crabshell Blue into the fighting bowl.

The two crickets flew at each other, chirping defiantly. The small one jumped high, landed on the other's neck, and bit hard.

Fearing his champion would be killed, the magistrate snatched Crabshell Blue away. The red cricket sang a victory song.

That day, the little red cricket—who was Wei nian—left for the imperial city in a bamboo cage. It was a long journey. Wei nian had never imagined the world could be so big.

Soon after arriving at the emperor's palace, Wei nian was matched against the court champion, Longwings, a seasoned fighter twice his size. Wei nian was too frightened to move, even though he heard the courtiers laughing. Someone hit his antennae with a boar's bristle. It felt like a sharp stick.

The big cricket lunged at him, biting his front leg. The pain made Wei nian explode into action. He still had his own wits, though he lived in a cricket's body.

Wei nian gathered his strength and leaped over his opponent. The big cricket slammed against the side of the bowl, rolled over, and came at him again. Wei nian dodged and bit the champion below its wing. It twisted and turned, lunged again and again, but it couldn't catch Wei nian. He attacked it with quick bites.

Exhausted and confused, Longwings retreated toward the rim of the fighting bowl and cowered there, trembling.

Once more the little cricket warrior sang his victory song.

So Wei nian became the court champion, defeating challengers from every province. When he heard the music of lutes and zithers played to celebrate his victories, he danced to the beat. He feasted on crabmeat and chestnuts, drank the sweetest spring water.

Still he longed for home. He wanted to sit beside his mother, to run on two legs under open sky. One night, when a careless servant left the door of his golden cage ajar, Wei nian escaped. The moon helped him find his way among the royal pavilions.

At daybreak the small red cricket, battered and weary, crawled across the courtyard beside the palace kitchen, trying to find a crack in the outer wall. He did not think he had the strength to make his way through the great city beyond the palace, but he knew he had to try.

Then he heard a terrible noise. A flock of chickens was looking for food. One stretched out its neck to peck at him. It missed. Weakly, he jumped away. It covered him with its claw. Mustering all his strength, Wei nian pushed up between the chicken's toes and flew to its head, holding on with his pincers.

Frantically, the chicken tried to shake him off. It was even more frightened when a shadowy figure shimmered against the palace wall. The old man gently lifted the tired little cricket into the fold of his sleeve.

"You have been an honor to your family," the old man whispered.

When the little red cricket had become famous, everyone in Cheng Ming's village had celebrated. The grateful emperor had canceled their taxes for five years. He also had rewarded the magistrate with gold, bolts of silk, a string of fine horses. In turn, the magistrate had canceled Cheng Ming's debts and given him a flourishing orchard instead of his dried-up fields.

Cheng Ming and Li hua had not joined the celebrations. Every evening, Cheng Ming wept as he gathered the finest pomegranates from the orchard to place before the portraits of his ancestors. "I would give up everything to have my son back," he vowed.

One night, Cheng Ming and Li hua heard a quick sweet "Chir-rup, chir-rup, chir-rup!" coming from the garden. Reminded of the little red cricket, Cheng Ming went to the doorway to listen. There in the moonlight stood Wei nian.

Cheng Ming and Li hua opened their arms to welcome their son.

"How did you get this awful scar?" Li hua asked, stroking his arm.

"In a fight. I won!" Wei nian grinned and showed his muscles. Suddenly Cheng Ming remembered the small red cricket waving its antennae and chirping fiercely.

"*You* were the cricket warrior," he said.

Wei nian smiled and bowed his head.

Cheng Ming and Li hua thanked their ancestors for returning their son, their greatest treasure, to them. Wei nian went to school and in time he became an accomplished calligrapher, famous throughout his province for loyalty to his family, for his delicate poetry, and for his lifelike paintings of crickets.

THE CRICKET WARRIOR

"The Fighting Cricket" was first recorded by Pu Songling (1640–1715), a writer and teacher who collected tales of magic and the supernatural told by people of his native Shandong (Shantung) province. Selections from his collection, one of the most popular books in China, were first translated into English with the title *Strange Stories from a Chinese Studio* by Herbert A. Giles in 1908. We have created our own version of Pu Songling's satirical tale about the suffering caused by an emperor's whim, focusing on elements common in Chinese folklore—magical transformation and family loyalty.

Margaret and Raymond Chang